ASHA and BAZ
Meet Mary Sherman Morgan

ASHA and BAZ
Meet Mary Sherman Morgan

(Book 1)

By Caroline Fernandez

Common Deer Press

Published in 2022 by Common Deer Press
1745 Rockland Avenue
Victoria, British Columbia
V8S 1W6

This book is a work of fiction. All incidents and dialogue, and
all characters, with the exception of some well-known historical
and public figures, are products of the author's imagination and
are not to be construed as real. Where real-life historical or public
figures appear, the situations, incidents, and dialogues concerning
those persons are entirely fictional and are not intended to depict
actual events or to change the entirely fictional nature of the work.
In all other respects, any resemblance to persons living or dead
is entirely coincidental.

Library and Archives Canada Cataloguing in Publication

Title: Asha and Baz Meet Mary Sherman Morgan /
by Caroline Fernandez.
Names: Fernandez, Caroline (Blogger), author.
| Patel, Dharmali, 1981— illustrator.
Description: Illustrated by Dharmali Patel. | "Book 1".
Identifiers: Canadiana (print) 2021036954X
| Canadiana (ebook) 20210369558 | ISBN 9781988761671
(softcover) | ISBN 9781988761688 (PDF)
Classification: LCC PS8611.E7495 A92 2022 | DDC jC813/.6—dc23

Cover and interior illustrations: Dharmali Patel
Book Design: David Moratto

Printed in Canada
CommonDeerPress.com

In honour of Mary Sherman Morgan
and all women in science and technology
who overcome challenges
to make amazing discoveries.

For my amazing daughter Kaavya!

CHAPTER 1

THE GREAT ROCKET CHALLENGE

The science class was abuzz with brainstorming the best ways to build a paper rocket. Kids sat in pairs on the floor, on desks, even out in the hall, as they worked together on their rockets. Ms. Wilson, the science teacher, went from group to group checking on their progress.

"How do we launch the rocket into the air?" Asha asked her best friend Baz. "We need the rocket to launch out . . . not up." Baz chewed on his lip as he always did when he was trying to sort out a problem.

"Any questions?" Ms. Wilson asked Asha and Baz when she popped by their spot in the corner of the room. All the kids thought Ms. Wilson was the best teacher in the school because she came up with fun class projects.

"No questions. We're good." Asha replied quickly.

Baz felt uncomfortable being put on the spot. He just stayed quiet and tried to blend in with the wall.

The Great Rocket Challenge was a project and a competition. The teams had to make a paper rocket fly the farthest. However, the challenge was that they could only pick their rocket supplies from eight items:

- **white computer paper,**
- **tape,**
- **scissors,**
- **paper straws,**
- **glue,**
- **pencils,**
- **cardboard rolls, and**
- **markers.**

The team with the rocket that flew the farthest would meet Chris Hadfield, the Canadian astronaut, at the school assembly! Asha and Baz wanted their rocket to be the one that flew the farthest. They wanted to win the rocket competition.

"Ours is going to be better than yours!" bragged the team nearest to Asha and Baz.

"Pfft . . . not possible! Do *you* have Baz on your team? No, *you* don't," Asha shot back. Everyone knew Baz was the smartest kid in science class. He was amazing in math and problem solving. Asha, on the other hand, was creative and curious. She was definitely the most outgoing in the class.

Asha and Baz were best friends and always picked each other for partners. They even had a plan to be partners when they grew up. Baz would be an animal biologist and Asha would be a teacher. They would travel the world together teaching people about saving animals.

Asha and Baz looked around the class. Some teams were using the cardboard rolls as rocket bodies.

"Too heavy," said Baz.

Other teams were using glue to attach paper straws together.

"Too messy," said Asha.

A few teams were making paper airplanes.

"Not even rockets!" Baz whispered.

Asha and Baz brainstormed a different way to build a rocket. They decided to make a light yet solid rocket using only three items for construction: paper, a pencil, and tape.

They cut a rectangle of paper to be the rocket body. They rolled the paper snugly around the pencil and taped it to itself. Then, they folded over the top of the paper to make a rocket nose cone. Finally, they cut three small triangles to attach to the bottom as rocket fins. Carefully, they slid the paper rocket off of the pencil. Success. It looked like a real rocket!

Launching the rocket was their roadblock.

"What if we connected the bottom of the rocket to the top of my water bottle and then squirted water through it?" Baz suggested. "The water would create energy to blast the rocket."

"Wouldn't the water soak the paper?" Asha wondered.

"True," said Baz.

"Wet paper can't fly," said Asha. "Plus, water isn't on the supply list anyway."

Baz looked stressed.

"Keep thinking," Asha encouraged.

Baz looked around at the teams and chewed on his lip. Some were already testing their rockets. "We are falling behind," said Baz.

"We'll figure it out. Don't worry," Asha said, trying to boost his spirits.

"Start cleaning up. It's time for lunch,"

Ms. Wilson said cheerfully. "After recess you can continue working on your rockets."

Asha and Baz cleaned up the rocket supplies.

"Since it is so nice out," Ms. Wilson announced, "you can have lunch outside."

The kids clapped all at once. Lunch outside was a treat. Ms. Wilson really was the best teacher!

The bell rang out and everyone went outside. Groups of kids sat together on the playground eating, talking, and playing.

Asha and Baz headed to the edge of the playground, where the grass turned into sand.

"So how do we get our rocket to launch?" Asha asked as she plopped on the ground and took out her thermos and fork. She quickly dug into her delicious curry, enjoying every bite.

"Let's talk out the problem," Baz suggested. He loved planning. Baz sat next to Asha and began munching on his plain cheese and butter sandwich with the crusts cut off. "We need our rocket to go the farthest. For it to fly, we need energy. Something to push it across the classroom," Baz said in between bites.

"And water can't do that," said Asha pointing her fork in the air.

"Right. We need to use something on the supply list. But also something that won't break the rocket," said Baz.

"Correct," Asha replied, then swallowed.

They finished their lunches and wiped their mouths with the backs of their hands. They put their containers back in their lunch bags and put their lunch bags on the grass.

Just then, Asha noticed an extraordinary stick lying in between the sand and grass. It wasn't rough and covered in bark like all the other sticks in the schoolyard. This stick looked as if it had been polished by someone. It was as long as the length between Asha's wrist and elbow. The wood was a dark chocolate brown at one end that flowed into a warm honey yellow at the opposite tip. This unusual piece of wood also had an interesting bend to it. Asha and Baz were both drawn to the odd stick.

"Wow, look at this!" Asha declared picking it up.

"Can I hold it?" Baz asked.

"Just a minute," Asha replied holding up her hand like a stop sign. "I know just what to do with this stick ... let me draw our rocket."

Asha bent down to the sand and drew the outline of their rocket. First a nose cone at the top, then a body tube in the middle. Finally, she drew three rocket fins at the bottom.

"Get in!" Asha invited Baz.

Asha and Baz stepped into the rocket ship. Asha touched the stick to the sand as if she were pressing a button. "Blast off!" she yelled. In that exact moment, the south wind blew sand into a gentle tornado around them. Asha and Baz were transported through space and time.

"What was that?!" Baz exclaimed as the mini tornado died out.

"Magic?" Asha guessed.

"On second thought, never mind," Baz said taking a few steps back in fear. "I don't want to hold the stick after all."

"Look," Asha said pointing down to the sand. "The rocket is gone."

The rocket ship drawing had disappeared with the tornado, and written in its place was a name and a year:

MARY SHERMAN MORGAN. 1957.

CHAPTER 2

1957 CALIFORNIA, USA

"Let's go back. We should go back." Baz was worried. "Wait . . . how do we go back?"

"We go back the same way we came," Asha said with confidence. "We draw something in the sand and touch the stick to the ground. Don't worry. I'll take care of it."

"OK, but you hold the stick when we go back," Baz suggested. He was already planning their return.

"Baz, this is a magic wand. We found a magic wand!"

"I'm not sure a magic wand is such a good idea. . . . "

"Where are we?" Asha asked, ignoring Baz's worry.

Baz looked around. On the ground, the sand met concrete where before it had met grass. He looked into the distance and to his surprise their school was gone. Instead, he saw planes parked outside an airplane hangar. It looked like a factory of some sort. There was a sign on top of the building.

"North American Aviation," Baz read, surprised.

"Aviation?" Asha asked.

"Aviation might have something to do with airplanes and flying." Baz guessed. "They must build airplanes here."

As they walked closer to the hanger, they realized these weren't regular airplanes.

"Maybe it's connected. Aviation. Airplanes. Rockets. What if the magic wand brought us here to help with our project?" Asha wondered.

She put the magic wand in her pocket to keep it safe.

"The magic wand wrote Mary Sherman Morgan in the sand," Baz added. "Maybe we need to find Mary Sherman Morgan."

"Let's go!" Asha led the way. The two kids walked up the runway and in between the planes.

"I've seen planes before, but they didn't look anything like this one," Asha commented.

"That's a fighter jet. I've seen pictures of them in history books. Fighter jets only held the pilot," said Baz.

It was true. There was only one seat in the

plane. There was a glass bubble top where the pilot could look out. The fins, body, and wings of the plane were made of gray steel. There was a blue star and red stripes painted on the body of the plane just below the pilot's door.

"Watch out!" yelled a man wearing denim overalls.

Asha and Baz looked toward him and saw a different kind of plane slowly rolling down the runway. Its propeller whirled round and round on its nose. The kids moved to the side and gave room for the propeller plane to pass them. The pilot nodded his head and waved to them as he passed.

"Do you think we should hide?" Baz worried.

"Why would we hide?" Asha replied, confused.

"Because we're kids, and children probably aren't allowed to be here," Baz replied, chewing his lip.

"We aren't kids." Asha laughed. "We're rocket scientists!"

And that was that. They were rocket scientists, in 1957, at North American Aviation.

"Let's go find Mary," Asha suggested, tapping Baz on the shoulder. "This way!"

They walked through the huge hangar doors. It was like a garage for airplanes. There were rows upon rows of planes parked inside. Rolling ladders with platforms stood beside the planes. Mechanics worked on fighter jet engines and propeller planes. Big metal lights hung down from metal beams in the ceiling.

"Do you see anyone who looks like a Mary?" Asha asked Baz.

The mechanics and pilots were all men.

"Maybe up there," suggested Baz. He pointed to windows at the back of the building.

It seemed there were offices above the

hanger. The kids found a door marked STAIRS. They opened the door and walked up to the second level. They opened another door and walked into a hallway. They were right. Offices!

It was full of men with dark suits, white shirts with buttons, and black ties. Some sat on their own at desks reading over papers. Others stood in groups of two or three talking over projects.

All of the furniture was made of steel like the airplanes downstairs. Steel desks. Steel chairs. Steel cabinets. Some of the desks had metal filing trays. Others had metal typewriters. A few had big metal machines with push-button numbers on them. Asha walked up to one of the strange machines.

"What is this?" Asha asked with curiosity. She pushed down on a number button. CLICK was the sound it made. This strange machine had addition, subtraction, multiplication, and division buttons on it. Asha pressed another number button. CLICK. And then she pressed the multiplication button. CLICK. All of a sudden, the machine started making whirling noises. Numbers rolled through a dial.

"I broke it!" moaned Asha.

"No. It's multiplying the numbers. It's a calculator!" said Baz.

"A big, loud, 1957 calculator," said Asha. "What if I press this?" Asha stretched out her hand to press another number button, but Baz stopped her.

"Focus. We are here to find Mary," he reminded her.

"Right!" Asha responded. "I forgot."

"Anyone here look like a Mary to you?" Baz asked. He only saw men as far as his eyes could see.

"Let's ask someone," suggested Asha.

And before Baz could stop her, she tapped a man's arm. The man was wearing a janitor uniform. He was pushing a cart filled with mops, brooms, and cleaning supplies. On the pocket of his uniform was a name tag that read JOE.

"Excuse me, Joe, ahem. . . . " She cleared her throat. "We are new rocket scientists here. Could you tell us where to find Mary Sherman Morgan?"

"Well, that's easy," Joe replied in a rude tone

of voice. "You can't miss Mary, she's the only woman working on rockets on the engineering floor."

"She works on rockets?" Asha asked.

"That's what I hear!" said Joe. "She's over there." He pointed toward the only woman in the room. She was sitting at a desk in the farthest corner of the office.

Mary Sherman Morgan was a thin woman in her 30s. She had short, wavy, brown hair. She wore a light-green, short-sleeved dress with buttons running down the front. When they got closer, Baz could see she had warm brown eyes behind dark-framed glasses.

She sat quietly at her desk punching numbers

into one of the calculator machines. Mary used a pencil to write the calculations down on a paper. She was very focused on her work.

"Excuse me?" Asha asked.

The lady looked up from her papers.

"We are rocket scientists," Asha continued, "and we are looking for Mary Sherman Morgan."

"I'm Mary. How can I help you?" Mary replied with a warm smile.

"Our rocket," Baz broke in. "We need your help with our rocket."

CHAPTER 3

THE SPACE RACE

"**I** would really like to help, but I'm already working on a rocket project," Mary replied.

"We just need help with the launch part," said Baz.

"That's exactly my problem with this rocket!" Mary sighed. She tapped her pencil on her notes in frustration. "Launching a rocket is challenging."

"Don't try to launch it with water," said Baz. "We considered using water to power our rocket, but we decided it wouldn't work."

"No, water definitely won't work" said Mary,

smiling. "Our rocket has to be powered by a chemical mixture. But what chemicals make the right combination?" she asked.

Mary looked back down at her paper and then punched a few more numbers into her calculator. A moment later, she looked back at the kids.

"Those desks over there are free," she said pointing to desks beside hers. "Perhaps you will solve your launch problem before I solve mine."

"Thanks, Mary," Baz said. He sat on one of the metal chairs.

Baz motioned to Asha to sit on the chair beside him. He whispered in her ear, "Maybe Mary can't help us with our rocket."

Asha whispered back, "Why would you think that?"

"She seems to be as stuck as we are," said Baz.

"The magic wand can't be wrong. Mary Sherman Morgan knows how to launch a rocket," Asha replied with confidence.

"Let's go men! And lady." A man clapped his hands together as he walked into the room. "We need to win the space race!" He wore a gray suit and a white button-up shirt with a black tie and had short brown hair.

"The lady is working on it, Roger," Mary said to Roger when he stopped at her desk.

"Space race?" Asha asked.

"The race to space. Between us and the Soviets," said an engineer who was sitting at a gray desk to the right of Asha and Baz. The man looked similar to Roger, except this man wore a sweater, brown tie, and black glasses.

"Hi! I'm Pete. You must be new here," Pete said to Asha. He stretched his arm to shake Asha's hand. "The Soviets have already launched their satellite into space. They named it Sputnik."

"Sputnik?" Asha asked.

"That's the name," said Roger. He sat down at his desk, which was in front of Pete's.

"They launched it into orbit earlier this year on October 4th," said Pete.

"The space race has started and we are already behind," Roger moaned.

Roger looked at a blueprint of a rocket that was taped to Mary's blackboard. He shook his head side to side. It appeared he didn't like to be in last place.

"There are currently two great powers in the world. The Soviet Union and the United States of America. And we are competing to be the greatest! Each of us wants to be better than the other. Better. Smarter. Richer. Stronger," said Pete.

"They've got a head start, so we have to take the lead in the next stage of the space race. We have to get our own satellite into orbit!" said Roger.

"Why does it have to be a race?" Asha asked.

"Because the winner of a race is the best. And we want to be the best," said Roger.

"Like us wanting our rocket to go the farthest in front of Chris Hadfield," Baz whispered.

Asha nodded in agreement. She knew what it felt like to want to be the best. "It's a rocket competition," she said.

"Exactly," said Roger. "And we've got the rocket. She's a beauty." He pointed to the rocket on the blueprint. "Let me introduce you to the Jupiter-C rocket."

The kids looked at the drawing of the Jupiter-C rocket. The rocket was long and thin. It appeared to be made of metal that was painted white. USA was written down the body of the rocket in big letters.

"Jupiter? Like the planet Jupiter?" Baz asked.

"Yes, the planet Jupiter, the biggest planet in our solar system!" said Roger.

"It looks like our rocket," Asha whispered to Baz.

"The problem is, how do we power it to lift off?" Pete asked out loud.

"We have a power problem on our rocket too," Baz said. "Is the space race done when you launch the Jupiter-C rocket?"

"No way!" replied Roger. "I hear the Soviets are thinking about sending a dog up into space in a rocket. Can you imagine that? Sending a dog?!"

"Who would send a dog to space?" exclaimed Pete. "That's silly."

"If they send a dog, we'll do better. We'll send a man into space!" Roger predicted.

"And who knows? Maybe we'll get a man on the moon!" replied Pete.

"Or one day, maybe a man will live in space!" said Roger.

"Gentlemen," said Mary looking up from her desk. "There will be no dogs or men, in space or on the moon, until we launch this rocket. Let's not get ahead of ourselves."

The two men looked as if their teacher had told them to stop talking. They settled into their seats and began silently reading.

Asha and Baz looked over at Mary. She had stood up and was writing on a large blackboard with white chalk.

"What are you doing, Mary?" Baz asked.

"I'm making a list for the Jupiter-C rocket.

I have determined there are certain things required to launch the rocket."

Baz and Asha looked on the blackboard where Mary had written her list. She had written:

- **AVAILABILITY**
- **DATA**
- **PRESSURE**

Baz looked at the points. "I get it," he said. "It's just like our rocket. For availability, we had to stick to the rocket supplies Ms. Wilson gave us. The paper, tape, straws, and stuff."

"Yes, the supplies used to launch a rocket must be available in large quantities. Because you don't just need the supplies for the rocket launch, you need them for the tests too," said Mary.

"And the rocket tests create data," Baz said.

"For example, if we had used water to power our rocket, it would have gotten the paper all wet," said Asha.

"And launch would have failed," added Baz.

"Exactly," said Mary. "Data tells us if something will work or not. For this rocket, we need to determine how to create enough pressure to boost it off the ground. Will the chemicals be stable when they are mixed together? What combinations of chemicals will create enough power to lift a rocket? The answers to these questions create data, which is needed to solve the power problem."

"I still don't get why they put a woman in charge of the rocket fuel," muttered Joe as he pushed his janitor cart by the desks. "Everyone knows girls can't launch rockets."

CHAPTER 4

GIRLS CAN'T LAUNCH ROCKETS

"**G**irls can so launch rockets!" Asha snapped back at Joe the janitor. He ignored her and kept pushing his cart around the rows of desks.

Asha balled her hands up and gritted her teeth.

"Don't listen to him," Baz advised Mary and Asha.

"Girls can do anything," Asha said to Baz.

"Hey, don't look at me. I'm on your team!" Baz reminded her.

"Anyone can do anything, if they put their mind to it," Mary replied.

"You must have done a lot of school to be a rocket engineer!" Baz said to Mary, trying to change the subject.

"I didn't finish school," Mary confessed as she looked at her blackboard. "Because, like many other women, I left school and went to work during the war."

"You helped in a war?" Baz asked. "Which war?"

"World War II," Mary explained, looking at Baz and Asha. "Before the war, it was usually men who had paid work and women who stayed at home to cook and clean and look after children. But when the men went to war, women had to go to work outside the home. There were jobs that needed to be done. Farm work, factory work, and science work," Mary explained.

Mary took out a package of cookies from a drawer in her desk and offered the snacks to the kids, Roger, and Pete. They each took a cookie. Mary then took one for herself before putting the package back in her desk drawer. They each bit into their cookie, which tasted like butter and vanilla.

"I studied chemistry in college" she explained. "But, when the war broke out, I was offered a chemistry job working in a factory. It was top secret at the time, but I can tell you now. I helped to create explosives for the military. After the war ended, I was offered a job here at North American Aviation."

"That's pretty fancy!" Baz said, impressed.

"Not bad for someone without a college education," Pete volunteered.

"If you had a degree, they'd pay you what a man earns," Roger teased.

"You get paid less than the men?" Asha was shocked.

"That's not fair," Baz said, shaking his head.

However, Mary didn't look sad. Instead, she appeared focused on her fuel problem. "What am I missing?" Mary whispered to herself, turning toward the blackboard. She looked at the white chalk numbers, arrows, and chemical names.

"Baz," Asha whispered, "let's leave her alone to think for a bit." Asha thought Mary needed thinking space.

The two children walked along the rows

and rows of desks. It was as if the desks were all soldiers standing at attention. Asha and Baz stood up a little taller. This was a place where there was no fooling around.

The kids walked past a corner office where they overheard two men having a discussion, a very loud and angry discussion.

"Listen Stan, you think you know your people, but I'm telling you, we can get someone better than that girl for this project!" said an older man in a blue military uniform. He had a rainbow of patches over one pocket of his jacket. His hair was short and he wore army boots. He was standing on the visitor side of a big steel desk. Sitting on the other side of the desk was a middle-aged man wearing square glasses.

"Hang on a minute," Asha whispered with concern to Baz. "They're talking about Mary." Asha tiptoed to the side of the door so the men wouldn't see her. She pressed her body tight to the wall. Baz tiptoed up beside her and stood flat against the wall.

"C-Colonel, with respect," Stan stuttered. "I do know my people. I'm telling you, Mary

Sherman Morgan is the best person for this job." Stan was sweating.

"I don't believe," the Colonel said, slapping his hand on Stan's desk, "that out of the nine hundred male engineers who work here, NINE HUNDRED MEN, you choose a woman to lead our biggest project!" The Colonel gave Stan a dirty look. "Women have no business playing around in science!"

Asha felt a bolt of hot anger shoot up her body. "He did *not* just say that!" She was about to storm into the office and give that man a stern talking to when Baz grabbed her arm and stopped her.

The Colonel continued talking in a raised voice. "Maybe you don't realize the situation, Stan. The Soviets are winning! We need to get a rocket into space and we need it done now!"

The Colonel's face was red with anger. He made a fist with his hand and punched it down onto the desk.

Without warning, Stan stood up behind his desk. He leaned forward and put both hands on his desk. Then, he spoke in a very low and firm voice. The kind of low voice that Ms.

Wilson used when she was really, really mad at the class.

"Colonel, Mary Sherman Morgan is the best person in this entire building to solve the power problem," said Stan with confidence. "I choose Mary!"

The Colonel stood face-to-face with Stan. They had a staring contest. Finally, the Colonel grumbled, "You better be right." He knocked his fist on Stan's desk. "The United States of America will not come in last in the space race. Do you understand me?"

"Understood," Stan said.

Asha and Baz heard the Colonel move and start walking toward the door. They quickly jumped behind a cabinet and hid.

The Colonel marched past them and they held their breath. They didn't need to be afraid. He didn't turn his head to notice them. He only looked forward, marching down the hallway and through the doorway to the stairs.

Stan let out a deep exhale. Then, he walked over to the door to his office and closed it.

Asha turned to Baz. She was on the brink

of tears. "They don't think Mary can do it," said Asha.

"She can do it," Baz answered. "You heard that Stan guy. He said she was the best person for the job. The magic wand brought us here for her. She will do it! Don't worry, Asha."

CHAPTER 5

SOLVING THE POWER PROBLEM

Asha and Baz returned to Mary, Pete, and Roger's desk areas.

They looked at the drawings taped to the blackboard. That's when Baz noticed something.

"I'm confused. Are there two rockets going into space?" Baz asked looking at the drawings.

"One rocket," Pete said. He pointed to the Jupiter-C drawing.

"Then, what is this rocket?" Baz pointed to another rocket drawing stuck up beside the Jupiter-C drawing. "Is it, like, the Plan B rocket?"

"That's the satellite," Pete stood and pointed

to the second drawing. "Explorer 1 is the satellite that goes inside the Jupiter-C rocket."

Pete picked up two pencils and held them one on top of the other.

"Pretend these are Explorer 1 and the Jupiter-C," he explained. "And pretend this one is inside this one." He held up the pencils. "The Jupiter-C rocket launches with Explorer 1 inside. When the Jupiter-C reaches the right spot in space, it releases Explorer 1. Then the satellite orbits around the Earth." Pete demonstrated by launching the pencils from his desk and then separating them up in the air.

"It'll be the first American satellite ever," added Roger.

"So Explorer 1 is getting a piggyback from the rocket?" Asha asked, looking at the diagrams.

"Kind of like that," said Pete.

"Satellites can't get themselves into space," Roger explained. "They need the power of a rocket to get them into orbit. Gravity holds everything down here on Earth, so we put tons of fuel inside a rocket to give it enough power to create the energy needed to boost away from gravity and the Earth's surface. Once the rocket has broken through Earth's atmosphere, it can release the satellite."

"Then, the satellite circles around the Earth," said Baz as the piggyback image clicked in his mind. "The rocket and the satellite are a team."

"Exactly," said Pete. "The Jupiter-C is already designed and built. And it's heavy and big. It will take a lot of power to get it to break gravity. We can't change the rocket at this point. The only thing we can change is the fuel we use to get it off the ground."

"Maybe we need to change the way we look at the power," Mary said, standing to take a closer look at the blackboard.

"What do you mean?" Asha asked.

"We know we have to use LOX," Mary replied looking at her formulas.

"LOX?" Baz asked.

Asha, Baz, and Pete joined Mary at the blackboard.

"LOX. It's a nickname for liquid oxygen. L is for liquid and OX is for oxygen," Roger explained, standing up from his desk. He walked over and joined the others at the blackboard.

"What if we changed the way we think? Instead of using formulas we've already tried, perhaps we should try something new," Mary suggested.

"We aren't supposed to do anything new. The Colonel doesn't like new," Roger warned. He looked worried.

"Listen, we have been working on the power problem for months. Nothing is working. Let's look at the problem in a different way!" Mary said.

"What if we . . . ?" she said to herself.

"Sometimes I think out loud too," Baz confessed to Pete.

Mary started brainstorming with chalk on the blackboard.

She wrote numbers and symbols on the blackboard, erased some numbers, and then replaced them with new numbers. It was try and then try again. "If we put this at 50 percent . . . no wait 60 percent and then that at 40 percent . . ." Mary said, lost in her thoughts.

She stepped back and looked at the numbers on the blackboard.

She had something. She moved to her calculator and pushed the numbered buttons. Her calculator whizzed and buzzed.

She looked closely at the calculations.

"It works," she whispered to herself.

"I doubt it," Roger said, looking over her shoulder at the calculations. And then he looked closer. "It works!" Roger admitted, surprised.

"You created a new fuel, Mary!" said Pete.

"You should name it," Asha advised. "Then, it will really be your creation."

"Wouldn't it be funny if we called it Bagel?" laughed Mary.

"Bagel?" asked Roger.

"It can be a joke," Mary suggested. "It runs on LOX. Liquid oxygen. And we name the other side of the power source bagel. Get it? Bagel and LOX. Bagel like the bread and lox like the fish."

"No one is going to approve a rocket fuel named after a sandwich," groaned Roger.

"You know what this means?" Pete asked everyone.

"The Hill," Mary replied with a smile.

"The Hill," Roger echoed.

"We are going to the Hill!" Pete confirmed.

"The Hill?" Baz looked confused. "I don't think I want to go to the Hill," he hesitated.

"The Hill is where North American Aviation does fuel testing!" said Roger. "It's a hot, deserted spot in the middle of nowhere. There's nothing there but the ground and the sky. And that's where we are going!"

CHAPTER 6

FUEL TESTING AT THE HILL

"**M**ary can't come to the Hill," Stan announced to the team. He looked very, very uncomfortable.

"Of course I'm going to the Hill!" replied Mary, blowing off his comment. She began organizing the papers she needed for the rocket test.

"Women aren't allowed on the Hill," Stan confessed. This wasn't a threat. It was a fact.

"But I created Bagel. I have to see how it tests," Mary pleaded.

"The men will test it. And we will give you

the data to crunch the numbers," Stan said with regret.

Pete stood up for Mary. "She created it, Stan. It's her work. If Roger or I had come up with the chemical combination, we would be going to the Hill."

"It's Mary's Bagel. She should see her Bagel and LOX launch!" Asha said with anger.

"About that . . . " Stan scratched the back of his neck. "The Colonel rejected the name Bagel. He decided to name it Hydyne. Pronounced like high-dine."

"She doesn't even get to name it?" Baz growled.

Everyone looked at Mary with pity.

"I'm going to the Hill, Stan," Mary said, not taking no for an answer. She didn't yell or stomp, but she was firm. "I created it. I need to see the test in person, as it's happening. Not just read about it in a test report next week."

"You can't," Stan replied.

Mary crossed her arms and stood her ground.

"Get me on the Hill, Stan," she said confidently.

Stan took a deep breath. He looked at the team and then at Mary. "I'll make a few calls," he said reluctantly.

Stan turned and walked down the hall to his office.

"So Hydyne," Roger said turning everyone's attention back to the drawings of the rocket.

They looked at the Jupiter-C and Explorer 1 drawings.

"I don't care what they name it as long as it works," said Pete.

"It will work," Mary said with pride.

"I know it will." Asha smiled back.

Suddenly, Stan's door blew open and he walked quickly down the row of desks. He did not stop to talk.

"What are you doing standing around?"

Stan called out as he put his hat on his head. "We have to drive over to the Hill as soon as possible! Let's go team. And lady!" Stan called out.

"Mary can go?" Baz asked.

"Mary can go," Stan said quickly. "And we are going right NOW."

Pete, Roger, Asha, Baz, and Mary all stepped in line behind Stan. He led them out of the North American Aviation building and into a waiting truck. An army officer was in the driver's seat ready to set off to the rocket testing site.

In an instant, they were on the road.

The drive to the Hill was bumpy and hot. They rode out of the city and away from people, high up into the Simi Hills. All around them was a rocky mountain range with green grass and brown dirt. There was nothing for miles except for birds flying in the air and the odd bug crawling on the ground. It was the perfect place to test rockets.

Rocket testing was dangerous business. The rocket could explode, misfire, or catch fire. There were millions of ways it could end in disaster. And that was the whole point of testing the rockets. It was better to know what didn't work in a rocket test before learning about a failure during a real rocket launch.

At the Hill, Mary and the others had to stand behind a blast wall for protection from the rocket test. The blast wall was a thick concrete wall taller than any person. If there was a rocket explosion, it would shield anyone standing behind it.

Field workers loaded Mary's new fuel, Hydyne, into barrels, which were put onto a truck. They drove the chemical out to the test rocket and filled up its tank.

Mary tried to look around the wall at the test rocket to see the Hydyne being pumped into the fuel tanks.

"Goodness, woman!" Stan declared. "You are supposed to stay behind the blast wall." Stan pulled her back.

"Countdown: ten, nine, eight ..." a male voice rang out from a speaker system.

"This is it." Roger's eyes sparkled.

"Seven, six ..." counted the voice.

"Five, four ..." the voice on the speaker counted down.

"I don't want to be here," said Baz. He bit his bottom lip and closed his eyes.

"Yes, you do!" Asha assured him taking his hand in hers.

A rocket rumbled in the distance. The ground vibrated under their feet.

"Three, two, one," the voice on the speaker counted. "LIFTOFF!"

The rocket roared into the air.

"LIFTOFF!" Asha and Baz yelled together.

The rocket launched into the air with a thunderous fire pushing it up into the clear blue sky.

"Test is successful. Test is successful," declared the voice on the speaker.

The team shook hands and congratulated each other. Asha and Baz took extra time shaking Mary's hand. "You did it," Asha complimented her. "You created a new rocket fuel. You got to go to the Hill. You are going to go down in history as the rocket lady!"

"I don't know about going down in history," laughed Stan at Asha's comment. "It's not like the history books are full of women."

Mary did not find this funny. Neither did Asha or Baz.

"But seriously," Stan corrected himself, "great work Mary. Hydyne is a major breakthrough."

"Thank you, Stan," Mary said humbly.

"Looks like the Jupiter-C is going forward to a real launch!" Roger said giving the group a thumb's up.

"Let's get back in the truck. We need to get back to North American Aviation. We have a rocket launch to plan!" Stan announced.

"Mary will get credit for creating Hydyne, right?" Asha asked Stan as they walked to the truck.

"Get in the truck," Stan replied, looking

uncomfortable. Pete and Roger looked the other way. No one said a word on the hot, bumpy ride back to the city.

CHAPTER 7

NEWS CONFERENCE

Asha and Baz sat at Mary's desk in the North American Aviation building. They read the front page of the morning newspaper.

THE TIMES
America's most read newspaper

January 31, 1958

USA TAKES LEAD IN SPACE RACE WITH EXPLORER 1 LAUNCH

The United States of America has launched the Jupiter-C rocket and the first American satellite, Explorer 1, into space. The launch took place at Cape Canaveral, Florida, at 10:48 p.m. local time. 108 minutes after the launch, Explorer 1 was successfully released into orbit.

A FEW FACTS ABOUT THE JUPITER-C ROCKET

- **Length: 20 m (66 ft)**
- **Weight: 29,180 kg (64,200 lb)**
- **Thrust: 370,000 newtons (83,000 lb)**
- **Propellants: Hydyne and liquid oxygen**

At 2:00 a.m., the leaders of the project attended a news conference at the National Academy of Science in Washington, D.C.

The United States of America is now leading the space race.

Asha read with eyes wide open. "Are you kidding me?"

They were the only ones on the engineering floor. Everyone else was in the cafeteria celebrating the launch with cake and coffee. The kids could hear clapping and cheers echoing through the hallways.

They read the article once, twice, three times.

"Where is Mary's name?" Asha asked Baz. It wasn't there.

Mary walked up behind them and looked at the newspaper. "It worked." She smiled.

"But it's not fair!" Baz cried. "Your name should be in the news. You invented Hydyne. The rocket wouldn't have gotten off the ground if it wasn't for you!"

Mary walked over to the blackboard and picked up the dusty eraser. She took a deep breath and looked at her work. Then, she started slowly erasing the numbers and ideas relating to her rocket fuel, Hydyne.

"Why didn't they take a picture of you holding the model of the rocket? It should be your picture they are putting on the front page of the newspaper," Asha said, outraged.

"Why didn't they take a picture of you at the news conference?" Baz asked Mary.

"I wasn't invited to go to the conference. Or the launch," Mary said quietly. "I don't like having my picture taken anyway."

"What?" Asha replied disgusted.

"But you made it happen," Baz said with heat. "They have to say it was you."

Mary erased the final chalk marks. Then, she gently pulled the rocket and satellite blueprints off the blackboard. She held the drawings for the kids to see.

"It launched," Mary replied. "That is what people will remember."

"It's wrong." Asha broke into tears.

Mary put the rocket drawings away in a drawer in her desk and settled into her chair.

"We have my rocket power problem solved. Why don't we put our minds together and find a solution to your rocket trouble," Mary suggested to change the topic.

CHAPTER 8

DON'T GIVE UP

"**I** don't care about our rocket. I give up on rockets," Asha whimpered. Baz put his arm around his best friend and gave her a squeeze.

"We don't give up," Mary cheered. "We find solutions to our problems with focus and hard work. That is what we do. That is who we are. We are rocket scientists." She gave the kids an encouraging smile.

She stood once again and went to the blackboard. She picked up a piece of white chalk and turned to the children.

"What supply availability do we have for your rocket?" she asked.

Asha wiped her face with her hand. "Paper, tape, glue, straws, pencils, cardboard rolls," she began.

"No Hydyne or liquid oxygen!" Baz jumped in.

Mary wrote the supply list on the blackboard with chalk.

"What is your rocket design now?" Mary asked.

"We wrapped the paper around the pencil and taped it together to make a rocket body. Then, we slid it off the pencil. We made a rocket nose by folding the paper at the top end. And then, we made three triangular paper fins at the bottom," Baz explained. "It looks a little bit like the Jupiter-C rocket."

"Paper fins are a great idea! They give the rocket stability," Mary said. "And do we want to launch it high up into the air or out across the room?"

"Out across the room," Baz answered. "The rocket that travels the farthest wins."

"It's a race," Asha added.

"So we don't necessarily need height. We need distance." Mary noted, writing the needs on the blackboard.

"Which is lighter, tape or glue?" Mary asked.

"Tape," Asha answered.

"So we won't use glue. It will weigh it down," Mary declared. "And we know paper is lighter than cardboard, correct?" she asked.

"Correct," Baz agreed. "We are using paper because it's lighter."

"And what do we have to put inside our rocket to power it to launch?" Mary asked.

"The pencil?" Asha questioned.

"Which isn't a power source," Baz said.

"What can be a power source?" Mary asked.

"Electricity," Baz suggested. "Plug in a light and you can see in the dark."

"Keep going." Mary encouraged the brainstorming.

"Chemicals. Like Hydyne powering the Jupiter-C rocket," replied Asha.

"Sun energy from solar panels," said Baz. "Water energy like how the power plants at Niagara Falls generate electricity. Wind energy like the wind turbines we see when we drive on the highway. ... Hey, wait!" Baz pointed his finger up in the air. "I have an idea! We can use wind energy to power our rocket!"

"Wind?" Asha said with confusion. "We can't make wind."

"I think Baz is looking at the problem in a different way," Mary replied and handed the chalk to Baz. He stepped up to the blackboard and began to draw.

He wrote:

PENCIL + PAPER + TAPE = ROCKET on the blackboard.

"This is what we have so far," Baz explained.

"Right," Asha said.

"I'm following you." Mary nodded.

Then, Baz wrote:

ROCKET + STRAW + BLOWING = WIND POWER on the blackboard.

"Blow the straw inside the rocket," Asha exclaimed. "We can create wind energy!"

"Right? Am I right?" Baz asked Mary. "I'm right, aren't I?"

"It works," Mary said with a big smile.

"We solved our rocket power problem!" Baz said proudly.

"We have to get back to test our rocket. NOW!" Asha said excitedly.

They each gave Mary a great big hug and said their goodbyes.

They ran down the hall of the office floor, out the door, down the stairs, out of the North American Aviation building, and across the runway.

They ran all the way to where the concrete met the sand.

Asha took the magic wand out from her back pocket. She crouched down and made a drawing of their school in the sand.

"I hope this works," said Baz.

Asha and Baz stepped into the school drawing. Asha touched the magic wand to the sand like pressing a button. She yelled, "School!" In that exact moment, the south wind blew the sand into a gentle tornado around them. Asha and Baz were transported through space and time.

Just then, they heard the bell ring out. Lunch break was over. They ran to line up in their class lines. Then, they filed inside the school doors, one student by one student. They returned to the science classroom. Asha put the magic wand in her backpack to keep it safe.

They washed their hands with soap at the sink and returned to their workstations.

"Let's get ready to test our rocket fuel. Wind power!" Baz announced.

CHAPTER 9

LIFT OFF

Asha made a new rocket. She rolled the paper tight around the pencil and stuck it together with a piece of tape. At the bottom end, she taped on three rocket fins. Baz picked up a paper straw. It fit perfectly inside their paper rocket. He blew. The rocket didn't launch. It didn't even move off of the straw.

He was surprised with the rocket test failure.

"The nose!" Asha exclaimed. "We didn't fold over the nose at the top end of the rocket."

"So the air blew out the open end!" Baz realized.

"Let's try again," Asha suggested.

They made a second rocket. This time they folded the open end of the paper rocket into a nose cone and taped it down.

"Rocket test number two," Asha called out.

Baz took another paper straw and inserted it into the open end of the rocket. He took a deep breath and then blew out into the straw. The white paper straw rocket flew across the room.

"It works!" Asha cheered.

"Wind energy is our power source!" Baz said proudly.

Ms. Wilson, the science teacher, saw their successful launch. She walked over to the two best friends. "What did I just see?!" she exclaimed. "Do it again for the whole class."

Ms. Wilson invited Asha and Baz to stand at the front of the class. Baz handed the rocket to Asha and whispered, "be my guest." Asha took a clean paper straw from their supplies and inserted it into the end of the rocket.

"Let's count down," Ms. Wilson told the class. "Three, two, one," the class chimed together. "BLAST OFF!"

Asha blew into the straw with all her might. The paper rocket launched across the class and into someone's backpack at the back of the classroom.

The class broke into excited cheers and clapping.

"Settle down. Settle down," Ms. Wilson told the class. "Time is up on the Great Rocket Challenge project. We must vote. All in favor of Asha and Baz presenting their rocket to Chris Hadfield raise your hands."

Asha and Baz looked out into the class.

Every single student raised their hand into the air. Every. Single. Kid.

"You have everyone's vote, so it's agreed. You get to present your rocket at the assembly." Ms. Wilson congratulated them.

"Does anyone have any questions for Asha and Baz about their rocket?" Ms. Wilson asked.

Hands shot up all over the class. One by one students asked their questions.

"What are the fins for?" asked one boy.

"Why didn't you use cardboard?" asked a girl.

"How does the straw launch the rocket?" asked another boy.

Asha and Baz answered every question. They talked about their rocket design, the supply availability, testing, and their power source.

"One last thing for Asha and Baz," Ms. Wilson

said. "And this is for the assembly. Think about it and keep it a secret until your demonstration, so we will all be surprised."

"OK," Baz replied, a bit scared. He wondered what more they could need to do for this project. And why should it be a secret?

"What are you going to name your rocket?" Ms. Wilson asked. Asha and Baz looked at each other for name ideas. Asha stuck her finger in the air like she had an idea. She was about to say it when Ms. Wilson said "Shhh . . . don't tell us now." Ms. Wilson held her finger up to her closed mouth. "Announce the rocket name at the assembly."

Baz and Asha returned to their desks. Asha noticed Baz looked worried while they were cleaning up the rocket supplies.

"What's wrong?" she whispered.

"We have to come up with a name. And say it in front of Chris Hadfield and everyone," he said. "You know I don't like talking in front of an audience!"

"No problem. You know why? Because I LOVE talking. I'll be the talker and you be the rocket launcher," Asha said with a big smile.

"That sounds good to me," Baz answered, feeling relieved. "Deal!"

"And I know the perfect name for our rocket." said Asha. "Wait for it. . . . " She cupped her hand over her mouth and whispered into Baz's ear so that no one would hear.

"Perfect!" Baz did a double thumbs up when he heard the rocket name.

CHAPTER 10

MEETING CHRIS HADFIELD

In the school gym, two hundred kids sat cross-legged on the floor. At the front of the gym was a wooden stage raised off of the ground. The floor of the gym was concrete with painted lines for basketball and indoor hockey. Along the sides of the gym, there were wooden benches for the teachers to sit on. At the other end of the gym, there was a long wall and an emergency exit door.

Today, there was a line of parents standing against the back wall waiting to see a famous astronaut in real life.

Asha and Baz were surprised to find themselves on stage with the VIPs (Very Important People). Students never got to go on the stage! And the astronaut Chris Hadfield was up there with them!

Baz wanted to run away. He was sweating and he had butterflies in his tummy. Asha was thrilled to be on stage. She could have stayed there all day.

The gym was louder than usual for a school assembly.

Ms. Wilson picked up the microphone. She raised her hand up in the air. All the students and teachers raised their hands in the air as well. This was the signal to quiet down.

"Testing. One, two, three. Hello everyone," Ms. Wilson began. "As you know, we have a very special visitor. We are honored to have Chris Hadfield here with us today."

Everyone started clapping and cheering.

Chris Hadfield stood up and waved to the audience. His hair and mustache were the colors of the night sky. He wore a button-up shirt and a navy-blue suit. His eyes sparkled like stars.

There was a feeling that this was going to be the best assembly ever.

"Hands up if you know these Chris Hadfield facts," Ms. Wilson declared.

Chris Hadfield chuckled.

"Who knows Chris Hadfield grew up on a farm in Sarnia, Ontario?" she asked. Chris Hadfield put his hand up.

"Who knows that as a test pilot, Chris Hadfield has flown over seventy different types of aircraft?" she asked. A few people put their hands up.

"OK, this will stump you," the science teacher warned. "Who knows that Chris Hadfield was the first Canadian commander of the International Space Station, he did *two* space walks, and that he spent 160 days in space?" asked Ms. Wilson.

The students, teachers, and parents could not contain their excitement. Everyone cheered and clapped for Chris Hadfield. Ms. Wilson even made a whistle sound by putting her fingers in her mouth and blowing.

Chris Hadfield was the most famous person ever to visit their school. He was a real live astronaut.

Ms. Wilson raised her hand for the quiet signal. Slowly, the audience raised their hands as well and the room went quiet.

"Before I hand the microphone over to you, Colonel Hadfield, we have a demonstration."

Ms. Wilson turned to Asha and Baz. "Our rocket scientists," she said, introducing the kids, "will demonstrate a straw rocket launch."

Asha jumped out of her seat while Baz stayed glued to his. "I'll talk. You rocket launch," she whispered to him.

Baz nodded in agreement. The two walked to the front of the stage. Asha took the microphone from Ms. Wilson with confidence. Baz held the rocket out in his trembling hands.

"Hello, everyone." Asha stood with her shoulders back and her head held high. "I am Asha and this is Baz. We have a rocket to show you." She looked over to Chris Hadfield who watched them with interest.

With one hand, Asha held the microphone and with her other hand she pointed to details on the rocket as she explained the parts.

"You will see it has a nose cone, rocket body,

and fins. And it is powered by wind energy,"
Asha said. "And now, Baz will launch our rocket."

"The name!" Ms. Wilson whispered. "What
is your rocket's name?"

"Oh yes, the name!" Asha remembered. She looked at Baz with a big smile. "Our rocket is named Bagel."

And with that Baz inhaled deeply and then blew into the paper straw. The paper rocket flew out across the stage and into the audience. It landed on a boy's head in the fifth row.

"Can I keep this?" yelled the boy.

Everyone cheered.

Baz was so relieved his part was over! Asha felt like it was the best day ever.

Chris Hadfield walked over to the children and gave them each a high five. He leaned down so he would be eye to eye with the kids. He smelled like homemade maple syrup cookies.

"I have a question," he said to Asha and Baz. "Where did you get the inspiration to name your rocket Bagel?" he asked them.

Baz and Asha said together, "Mary Sherman Morgan."

"That works!" Chris Hadfield grinned. Then, he gave the kids another high five!

"Thank you, Baz and Asha," Ms. Wilson said. "That was a great demonstration!"

"And now . . . " she began. Everyone became silent. "Teachers, parents, students, Earthlings . . . let's give a warm welcome to Canada's astronaut . . ., Colonel Chris Hadfield."

Everyone applauded.

Chris Hadfield walked over and took the microphone from Ms. Wilson.

"Hello, I'm Chris. Chris Hadfield. And today I get to talk with you about science, space, and looking at things differently. . . . "

APPENDIX

Timeline of the Space Race Between the Soviet Union and the United States of America (1957–1969)

- October 4, 1957, Soviet Union: First satellite launch (Sputnik 1)
- November 3, 1957, Soviet Union: First animal on a spacecraft (a dog named Laika on Sputnik 2)
- February 1, 1958, USA: First American satellite (Explorer 1 powered by Hydyne and Liquid Oxygen)
- April 12, 1961, Soviet Union: First human in orbit (Yuri Gagarin on Vostok 1)
- February 20, 1962, USA: First American in orbit (John Glenn on Mercury-Atlas 6)
- June 16–19, 1963, Soviet Union: First woman in space (Valentina Tereshkova on Vostok 6)
- October 12, 1964, Soviet Union: First multi-person trip to space (Vladimir Komarov, Konstantin Feoktistov, and Boris Yegorov on Voskhod 1)

- March 18, 1965, Soviet Union: First space-walk (Aleksey Leonov on Voskhod 2)
- March 23, 1965, USA: First American multi-person spacecraft (Virgil Grissom and John Young on Gemini 3)
- June 3, 1965, USA: First American space-walk (Ed White on Gemini 4)
- December 15, 1965, USA: First orbital rendezvous in space (Frank Borman and James Lovell on Gemini 7 with Walter Schirra and Thomas Stafford on Gemini 6)
- February 3, 1966, Soviet Union: First soft landing on the Moon (Luna 9)
- March 16, 1966, USA: First docking in space (Neil Armstrong and David Schott on Gemini 8)
- September 14–21, 1968, Soviet Union: First spacecraft to fly around the Moon and return to Earth (Zond 5)
- October 11, 1968, USA: First crewed flight of Apollo program (Walter Schirra, Donn Eisele, and Walter Cunningham on Apollo 7)
- December 24, 1968, USA: First crewed flight around the Moon (Frank Borman, James Lovell, and William Anders on Apollo 8)

- July 20, 1969, USA: First humans to land on the Moon (Neil Armstrong and Buzz Aldrin on Apollo 11)

Was Mary Sherman Morgan a Real Person?

Though Asha and Baz's interaction with Mary Sherman Morgan is fictional, Mary was a real person. Here are some details about her life:

- Mary was born November 4, 1921, in Ray, North Dakota, in the United States of America.
- She grew up on a farm and did not go to school until she was nine years old.
- Mary was a good student and earned a scholarship to college.
- She left college two years before graduation, to go to work as a chemist at a weapons factory during World War II.
- Mary did not return to college to complete her degree in chemistry. Instead, she went to work at North American Aviation after the war.
- Mary was the only female working as a theoretical performance specialist at North American Aviation among nine hundred male engineers.

- Mary created the fuel to launch Explorer 1 and the Jupiter-C rocket into space.
- She considered naming the new fuel Bagel. Someone else decided to name it Hydyne.
- The news of Explorer 1 and the Jupiter-C launch made newspaper headlines in 1958. There was no mention of Mary Sherman Morgan in any of the news articles.
- Mary was a very private person and did not like being interviewed, nor did she like having her picture taken.
- Mary died August 4, 2004. She lived 82 years.

You can read more on the life and work of Mary Sherman Morgan in the book her son George Morgan wrote about her life: *Rocket Girl: The Story of Mary Sherman Morgan, America's First Female Rocket Scientist.*

Is Chris Hadfield a Real Person?

Yes, Chris Hadfield is a real person. Here are some facts about him:

- He was born on August 29, 1959, in Sarnia, Ontario, Canada.
- He was raised on a corn farm.
- He worked as an astronaut, engineer, and pilot.
- He was a commander, a Canadian Space Agency & NASA colonel, and a Royal Canadian Air Force fighter pilot.
- He is also an author, documentary series host, singer, and professor.

Visit www.chrishadfield.ca where you can read more on the life and work of Chris Hadfield.

What is the Soviet Union?

The Soviet Union is a short form for The Union of Soviet Socialist Republics (also known as the USSR). It existed from 1922 to 1991. Eventually, the Soviet Union broke up into separate countries, which are today's Russia, Ukraine, Armenia, and more.

Where Can I Learn More About Space?

These are reliable sources to learn more about space:

- National Aeronautics and Space Administration (NASA)
- European Space Agency (ESA)
- Canadian Space Agency (CSA)
- Non-fiction books
- Scientific magazines or news sites

Coming Next!

ASHA and BAZ
Meet Hedy Lamarr

(Book 2)
By
Caroline Fernandez

*Asha and Baz must crack the code
for the Great Coding Challenge!*

CHAPTER 1

THE CODING CHALLENGE

Almost every student group in the computer class was frustrated. Yet, there was a strong feeling of competition. They all wanted to be the first to solve *The Code Challenge*, but no one could crack it. Not even Asha and Baz, the most creative and smartest pair in the class, could figure it out.

THE CODE CHALLENGE:

Create a computer code to get a virtual frog from start point to finish point without falling off a log. The only way the frog can get across the water is to jump onto different size logs which float in different directions. If the frog misses a log, SPLASH! It falls in the water and it's game over.

Project partners took turns dragging and dropping code blocks from the coding menu into the code box:

The code blocks:
- **Hop Forward**
- **Hop Backward**
- **Hop Right**
- **Hop Left**

There were sounds of frustrated kids and game over sounds buzzing throughout the classroom.

GAME OVER.

"NO!" said a boy.

GAME OVER.

"What am I doing wrong?" asked a girl.

GAME OVER.

"Not fair," moaned another boy.

"This frog is broken," grunted the boy sitting at the computer next to Asha and Baz.

"You aren't doing it right!" growled his project partner. The boys elbowed each other in anger.

Asha and Baz felt discouraged too. They could not figure out the right code to guide their frog across the logs.

"What if we make all the code blocks Hop Forward blocks?" Asha suggested.

"OK. Let's try," said Baz. He felt a bit down. Usually he and his best friend did really well on projects.

He dragged and dropped all of the Hop Forward blocks into the code box.

Baz pressed the Try button at the bottom of the screen.

They both crossed their fingers and held their breath.

Their frog moved forward from the bottom of the screen onto a log. Good! Then, it hopped onto another log. Very Good! And then another. Excellent! Baz and Asha started to feel hopeful.

On the next Hop Forward block, there was no log in front of their frog.

SPLASH! GAME OVER.

"Come on!" Baz hit the desk with his fist.

"Ha ha," snarled the boy sitting beside them. "Have Baz the Brain and Asha the Amazing failed?" he said in a baby voice.

"Be quiet!" snapped Asha. The boy's teasing made her jaw go tight and heart pound.

At that moment, Ms. Wilson, their teacher, walked by their computer.

"No one is a loser," Ms. Wilson said looking straight at the boy. He shrunk down in his chair.

"What if we fail?" Baz asked Ms. Wilson.

"What if you succeed?" replied Ms. Wilson. She patted him on his shoulder. The encouraging touch made Baz feel a little better.

"Ms. Wilson, can you give us a hint on how to code the frog?" asked Asha. She hoped their teacher would take pity on them.

"Here's a good hint," said loudly to the class. Asha and Baz sat up in their chairs to hear. The boy next to them straightened up as well. "Don't give up!" said Ms. Wilson.

The class groaned. They had hoped their

teacher was actually going to give them a real hint on how to code the frog.

"You got this!" she cheered the class on as she continued walking from group to group.

Baz looked at their screen. The computer code was like a puzzle and they needed to fit the pieces together. He was usually so good at puzzles.

"What if we waited for all the logs to line up?" Baz suggested. "Then, there would be one straight path from start to finish."

They both leaned in and watched the screen for all the logs to line up.

They waited one minute. Two minutes. Three minutes.

Because the logs were different sizes and floated in different directions, they never all lined up at the same time.

"I give up!" Asha slapped her forehead and shook her head. "We are going to fail." She felt gloomy.

Just then, the recess bell rang.

"OK, everyone out for fresh air," Ms. Wilson called to the class. "You can come back to The Code Challenge after recess."

"Noooo," groaned the class. Everyone was fed up with The Code Challenge.

"Grab the magic stick," Baz whispered to Asha.

"It won't be any help," Asha grumbled. She felt defeated. But she went into her backpack and took out the magic stick anyway. It had been a helpful tool when brainstorming solutions to tough class projects before.

They walked out the computer lab door, down the hallway, and out the back door to the school yard. Once outside, they broke into a run and raced each other to the other end of the playground where the grass met the sand.

Asha got there first as she was the faster runner. Baz was just behind her.

"I don't want to do coding anymore. I give up. It's too hard." she said.

"I can't believe we haven't figured it out," said Baz. It was really bugging him that they couldn't get the code blocks in the right order.

"Maybe we just aren't smart enough," whispered Asha.

Baz pointed to the magic stick in Asha's hand.

"You remember what that does, right?" Baz asked.

They had found it in the schoolyard, and it certainly wasn't the sort of stick that just fell off a tree. It was polished and beautiful. And it had a strange wave in its shape. It was a dark chocolate color at the bottom that flowed into a honey color at the top. This was no ordinary schoolyard stick. This stick was magic.

The last time they drew in the sand with it, they had been transported to 1957 where they met Mary Sherman Morgan and learned about rocket power. Baz hoped it would do something similar this time.

"Draw in the sand, Asha," he instructed. "The code blocks. Maybe the magic stick will help us solve the code."

Asha bent down to the sand and drew a big square. Inside of it, she drew the blocks of code.

"Let's step inside," Baz said to Asha. "But maybe hold my hand," he said with a bit of worry.

Asha and Baz stepped inside the code drawing.

Asha crouched down and touched the magic stick to the sand. "Code," she said. In that exact moment, the south wind blew in and swept the sand up into a gentle mini tornado around their feet. In an instant, they traveled through space and time.

"Magic," said Baz.

"Look," Asha said pointing down to the sand. "The drawing is gone."

The code drawing had disappeared with the mini tornado, and written in its place was a name and a year:

HEDY LAMARR. 1941.

ACKNOWLEDGEMENTS

With thanks to Kirsten Marion, Dharmali Patel, Emily Stewart, and David Moratto for their talented contributions to the Asha and Baz series.

CPSIA information can be obtained
at www.ICGtesting.com
Printed in the USA
LVHW030224080922
727801LV00002B/312

9 781988 761671